P9-DHK-328

STERLING CHILDREN'S BOOKS
New York

An Imprint of Sterling Publishing
387 Park Avenue South
New York, NY 10016

STERLING CHILDREN'S BOOKS and the distinctive Sterling Children's Books
logo are trademarks of Sterling Publishing Co., Inc.

© 2014 by Sterling Publishing Co., Inc.
Design by Jennifer Browning

All rights reserved. No part of this publication may be reproduced, stored in a
retrieval system, or transmitted in any form or by any means (including electronic,
mechanical, photocopying, recording, or otherwise) without prior written
permission from the publisher.

ISBN 978-1-4027-8432-3

Distributed in Canada by Sterling Publishing
c/o Canadian Manda Group, 165 Dufferin Street
Toronto, Ontario, Canada M6K 3H6
Distributed in the United Kingdom by GMC Distribution Services
Castle Place, 166 High Street, Lewes, East Sussex, England BN7 1XU
Distributed in Australia by Capricorn Link (Australia) Pty. Ltd.
P.O. Box 704, Windsor, NSW 2756, Australia

For information about custom editions, special sales, and premium and corporate
purchases, please contact Sterling Special Sales at 800-805-5489
or specialsales@sterlingpublishing.com.

Printed in China

Lot #:
2 4 6 8 10 9 7 5 3 1
01/14

www.sterlingpublishing.com/kids

SILVER PENNY STORIES

King Arthur and His Knights

Told by Diane Namm
Illustrated by Marcos Calo

Once upon a time in the kingdom of Camelot, there ruled a good and wise king named Arthur.

There were also eight knights who lived in the different parts of the kingdom. The knights each had their own way of doing things, and they didn't get along. The first knight was a warrior. He wanted to go to war with his neighbors. The second knight was a peaceful man. He liked staying home to read quietly.

The third knight was too lazy to take care of his land. The fourth knight was too busy to take care of his land.

The fifth knight liked to travel and was never home. The sixth knight liked to play games and never did any work.

The seventh knight liked to sing and dance all day. And the eighth knight was tired of taking care of all of the other knights' duties.

Each knight thought his way was best.

Every day, one of them would complain to the king about the other knights. King Arthur listened to what each knight had to say.

"Will you help me, my king?" each one asked.

King Arthur replied, "Return home. I will think about what you have told me."

So the knights returned home to wait. Each knight expected the king to side with him.

King Arthur thought long and hard. He didn't sleep. He didn't eat. He paced up and down the royal hall until at last he had a plan.

"I shall invite all the knights to the palace to settle their differences," King Arthur told the beautiful Queen Guinevere over breakfast.

"We'll meet at this table!" he declared.

The next day, all the knights received a royal invitation to appear at King Arthur's court. Each knight believed the king would decide that his way was the right one.

As each knight arrived at King Arthur's castle, he was surprised to see the others there. Before they could begin to argue, King Arthur invited them in.

"Welcome, knights of Camelot,"
King Arthur said.

He showed them into the room with
the long, narrow table.

"Gentlemen, please have a seat,"
he said.

The first knight raced to the seat at the far end of the table, opposite the king.

"That's mine!" shouted the others.

Each thought he should have that important seat. Not one of them would sit, and they all kept shouting at each other.

"Silence!" commanded King Arthur.

The knights stopped fighting and listened to what the king had to say.

"Return in exactly one week," he commanded.

Grumbling, the knights left the castle. Again King Arthur thought long and hard. He didn't sleep. He didn't eat. He paced up and down the royal hall until at last he had another plan.

King Arthur summoned the royal carpenter. He explained exactly what he wanted. Soon the sound of sawing and hammering and sanding could be heard throughout the castle.

In exactly one week, the carpenter was done. King Arthur welcomed the knights again. This time, he showed them into a different room.

"Welcome to the first meeting of . . .

". . . the Knights of the Round Table!" King Arthur declared.

The knights saw that no seat was more important than any other one. One by one, they sat down at the round table.

"Now we can begin," King Arthur said to the knights.

The king and his knights talked for days. When they were done, each knight had been given the job that was best for him.

After that, the Knights of the Round Table worked together in peace. And the legend of King Arthur and his wisdom lives on to this day.